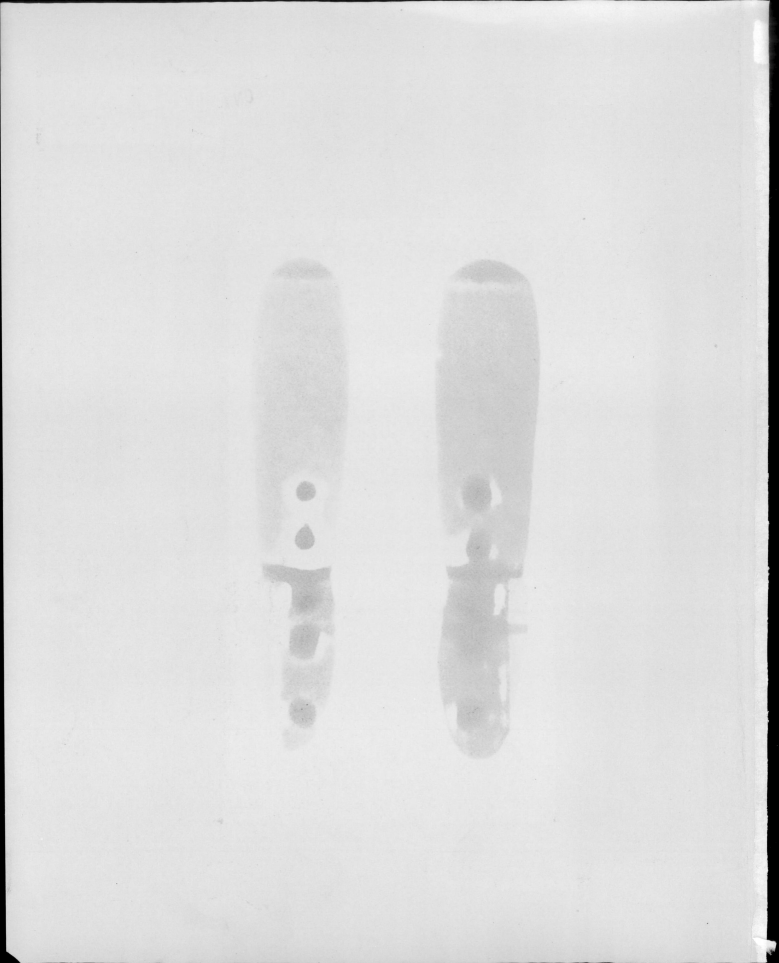

Jane R. Howard

WHEN I'M HUNGRY

illustrated by Teri Sloat

DUTTON CHILDREN'S BOOKS · NEW YORK

When I'm hungry and eat my breakfast,

sometimes I wish I could

eat my fruit right off the tree

or sip juicy nectar from a flower

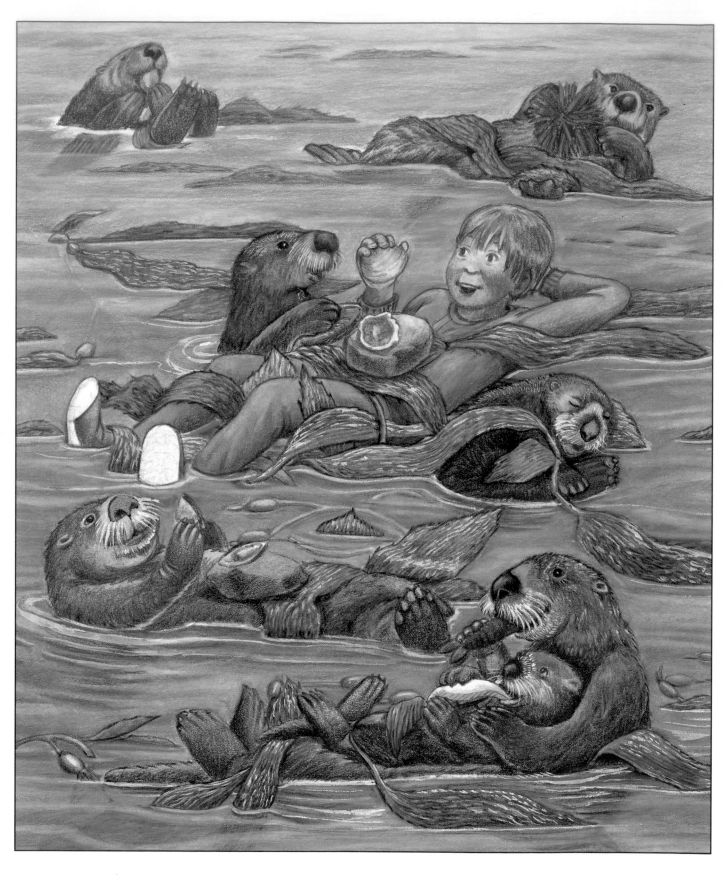

or float on my back with my food on my stomach

or maybe store it in my cheeks

or eat it underwater.

When I'm hungry for my morning snack, I wonder
how it would feel to lap with my tongue

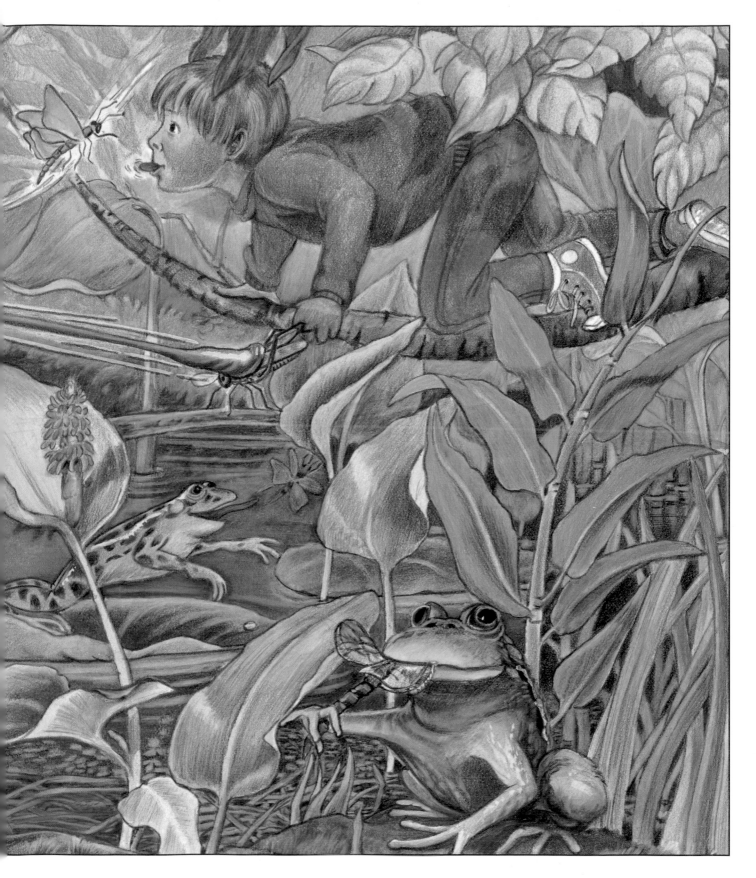

or use it to catch my food.

When I'm hungry, I sometimes think
I'd like to eat my lunch in the mud

or with my mouth wide open.

When I'm hungry in the afternoon,
I'm glad I don't have to dive for my food

or dig for wiggly worms

or get my honey from a tree.

And I'm glad I don't have to eat eucalyptus leaves

or bamboo shoots.

When I'm hungry at dinnertime, I'm happy to eat from my very own plate and drink from my very own glass,

right in the middle of my very own family.

To my sister,
Harriet Ruble Pritchard,
and her family,
for all their love and
enduring support.

J.R.H.

To my husband,
who is an artist, too.

T.S.

Text copyright © 1992 by Jane R. Howard
Illustrations copyright © 1992 by Teri Sloat

Library of Congress Cataloging-in-Publication Data

Howard, Jane R.
When I'm hungry / by Jane R. Howard;
illustrated by Teri Sloat.—1st ed.
p.   cm.
Summary: A child imagines eating like a variety of animals,
catching food or eating it off the trees, but decides that
using a plate and glass is best.
ISBN 0-525-44983-3
[1. Animals—Food habits—Fiction.   2. Food habits—Fiction.]
I. Sloat, Teri, ill.   II. Title.
PZ7.H83297Wg   1992
[E]—dc20
91-48164   CIP   AC

Published in the United States 1992 by
Dutton Children's Books,
a division of Penguin Books USA Inc.
375 Hudson Street, New York, New York 10014

Designer: Barbara Powderly

Printed in Hong Kong   First Edition
10 9 8 7 6 5 4 3 2 1